The Other Wise Man

The Other Wise Man

A Christmas Story by
Henry Van Dyke

Adapted by
Gabriel Bradford Millar

Illustrations & cover by
Terry Thomas

Hawthorn Press

The Other Wise Man © 1994, Hawthorn Press, Hawthorn House, 1 Lansdown Lane, Stroud, GL5 1BJ, U.K.

Typeset in Plantin by Saxon Graphics Ltd, Derby, U.K.
Printed in the United Kingdom.

British Library CIP data available on request

ISBN 1 869 890 663

The Other Wise Man

You know the story of the three Wise Men who came from the East to offer their gifts at the manger in Bethlehem. But have you heard the story of the fourth Wise Man who also saw the Star and set out to follow it? He did not arrive with the other three to honour the Child Jesus, but his was a long, strange journey. His tale was first told in the Hall of Dreams, in the Palace of the Heart of Humanity.

The Sign

It happened when Augustus Caesar ruled from Rome and Herod reigned in Jerusalem, a man named Artaban lived in the city of Ecbatana, among the mountains of Persia. From the roof of his house Artaban could look over to the hill where the summer palace of the Persian emperors glistened like a jewel in a crown.

Around the house of Artaban was a garden of flowers and fruit trees, watered by streams from the slopes of Mount Orontes, and made musical by many birds. But this soft September night there was only the sound of the water playing in the shadows. High above, through the curtained arches of the upper chamber, a dim light shone where the master of the house was meeting with his friends.

He greeted his guests at the door – a tall, dark man of forty, with brilliant eyes and firm, fine lips. He had the brow of a dreamer and the jaw of a soldier, a sensitive man with a strong will – one of those who, in whatever age they may live, are born for inward conflict and a life of quest.

His robe was of pure white wool, over a tunic of silk. It was the dress of the ancient priesthood of the Magi, whose element was fire.

'Welcome', he said in a low voice, as one after another entered the room – 'Welcome, Abdus; peace be with you, Tigranes, and with you, my father Abgarus. You are all welcome, and this house grows bright with the joy of your presence.'

There were nine, all in the rich silk clothes of noblemen, with winged circles of gold on their breasts, the sign of the followers of Zoroaster.

They took their places around a small black altar where a flame was burning. Artaban fed the fire with dry sticks of pine and fragrant oils. Then he began the ancient chant, and the voices of his companions joined in the hymn to the Great One, Ahura-Mazdao:

Shine on our gardens and fields,
Shine on our working and weaving,
Shine on the whole race of Man,
Believing and unbelieving

In the light of the fire the tiles of the floor shone bright blue. The windows were round arches hung with blue silk, and the ceiling was paved with sapphires, like heaven, with silver stars. The room was like a quiet starry night, blue and silver – it was as the house of a man should be – an image of the spirit of the master.

When the song was ended, Artaban said: 'As this fire is kindled, so our faith in the Great One is lit. This is His symbol, the purest of all created things. We have searched the secrets of nature together, and studied the healing powers of water and fire and the plants. But the highest of all learning is the knowledge of the stars. The stars are the thoughts of the Eternal. They are infinite.

But do not our books tell us that men will see the brightness of a great light, and He shall appear Who shall make life everlasting, and the dead shall rise again?

It has been shown to me and three others among the Magi – Caspar, Melchior and Balthasar – that this is the time of the coming of the newborn King. It falls in this year. We have studied the sky, and this night is the conjunction of two of the greatest stars. My three brothers are watching at the temple in Babylonia, and I am watching here.

If the Star shines again, they will wait ten days for me at the temple, and then we will set out together for Jerusalem, to see the Promised One who will be born King of Israel. I believe the sign will come, and I have made ready for the journey. I have sold my house and my goods and have bought these three jewels – a sapphire, a ruby and a pearl – to bring to the King. I ask you to go with me on this pilgrimage.'

While he was speaking he thrust his hand into a fold of his girdle and drew out three great gems — one blue as a piece of the night sky, one red as a ray of sunrise, and one pure as the snow of a mountain at twilight.

Artaban's friends looked on with cool eyes. A veil of doubt came over their faces, like a fog creeping up from the marshes to hide the hills. They glanced at each other with the looks of those who have been listening to a wild, impossible dream.

At last Tigranes said: 'Artaban, this is a vain dream. He who follows it is a chaser of shadows. Farewell.'

And another said: 'In my house there sleeps a new bride. I can neither leave her nor take her with me. So, farewell.'

But Abgarus, the oldest, and the one who loved Artaban the best, lingered after the others had gone and said: 'My son, it is better to follow even the shadow of the best than to remain content with the worst. And those who see wonderful things must often be ready to travel alone. I am too old for this journey, but my heart shall go with you day and night. Go in peace.'

So one by one they went out of the blue chamber with its silver stars, and Artaban was left in solitude. He gathered up the jewels and placed them in his girdle. Then he lifted the heavy curtain and walked under the arch, and out onto the terrace on the roof.

The sky was clear. The planets Jupiter and Saturn were so close together they became one light. Then a radiant white star moved in and pulsed with them, as though the three jewels in the Wise Man's breast had blended and become a living heart of light.

Artaban bowed his head. 'It is the sign', he said. 'The King is coming. I will go to meet Him.'

In the Grove of Date-Palms

All night long Vasda, Artaban's swiftest horse, had been waiting, saddled, in her stall, pawing the ground as if she shared her master's purpose.

Before the mist had lifted from the plain, and before the birds were singing their strong song, Artaban was in the saddle, riding swiftly along the high road, westward.

How close is the companionship between a man and his horse on a long journey! It is a silent friendship beyond the need of words. They drink at the same wayside springs and sleep under the same guarding stars. The master shares his evening meal with his companion – he feels the soft, moist lips caress the palm of his hand as they close over the piece of bread. At dawn he is roused by a warm breath on his sleeping face, and he looks up into the eyes of his fellow-traveller, ready for the adventure of the day.

And then, through the keen morning air, the swift hooves beat along the road, and the man and horse are moved by the same desire to devour the distance and reach their goal.

Artaban needed to ride swiftly to keep his appointment with the other Magi. He passed along the slopes of Mount Orontes, and across the plains where herds of wild horses bolted at his approach. At Baghistan he rode by the rich gardens watered by fountains from the rocks. He crossed the wind-swept shoulders of hills, and rode through more than one gorge where the river roared and raced before him like savage guide.

Through cold and desolate passes he and Vasda went undiscouraged. They crossed the foaming floods of the Tigris, through the vast city of Seleucia, built by Alexander the Great. They pressed on until they arrived at nightfall of the tenth day, beneath the walls of Babylon.

Vasda was exhausted, and Artaban would gladly have turned into the city to find rest and refreshment for them both. But he knew it was three hours journey yet to the temple where his comrades would be waiting, and he must reach the place by midnight. So he did not stop, but rode steadily across the fields.

A grove of date-palms made a dark island in which Vasda slowed down. She scented some danger or difficulty. It was not in her heart to fly from it, but to be prepared for it and meet it as a good horse would do. The grove was silent as a tomb; not one bird sang.

Vasda picked her way delicately, carrying her head low. Suddenly she stood shock-still, quivering in every muscle, before a dark object in the shadow of the last palm-tree.

Artaban dismounted. In the dim starlight he saw the form of a man lying in road. His humble clothes and the outline of his face showed that he was one of the poor Hebrew exiles who dwelt there. His skin, yellow as parchment, was that of one who had caught the fever of the marsh-lands in the autumn. Artaban felt the chill of death in his lean hand. He turned away, thinking that soon the funeral of the desert would begin, when the vultures and beasts of prey feast on the body, leaving only a heap of white bones in the sand.

But as he turned, a long, faint moan came from the man on the ground. The brown, bony fingers closed on the hem of his robe and held him fast.

Artaban's heart leapt to his throat, not with fear, but with dismay at this unforeseen delay. How could he stay here to take care of a dying stranger? If he lingered for even an hour he would not reach the meeting place at the appointed time. The other Magi would think he was not coming and they would go without him. He would lose the quest.

But if he went on now, the man would die. If he stayed, he might save him. Artaban's head pounded with the urgency of the crisis. Should he turn aside from following the Star, if only for a moment, to give a cup of cool water to a poor, dying Hebrew?

'God, direct me in the holy path, which thou only knowest!' prayed Artaban.

Then he turned back to the dying man. He lifted him up and carried him to the foot of a palm tree. He loosened the thick folds of the old man's turban and opened his robe. He brought water from a canal nearby and wet the man's mouth and brow. From his girdle he took a potent remedy that he always carried, and mixed it with the water, and poured it between the old man's lips. For the Magi were doctors as well as astrologers.

Hour after hour he laboured like a skilful healer, and at last the man's strength returned. He sat up and said:

'Who are you?' in the rough dialect of the land. 'Why have you brought back my life?'

'I am Artaban of Ecbatana, and I am going to Jerusalem in search of one who is to be born King of the Jews and Deliverer of all men. I dare not delay any longer, for the caravan is waiting for me and may now go without me. Here is all I have of bread and wine, and a potion of healing herbs. When you are stronger you can find the dwellings of the Hebrews in Babylon.'

The Jew raised his trembling hand to heaven: 'Now may the God of Abraham bless the journey of the merciful. I have nothing to give you in return – only this: I can tell you where the Messiah can be found. Our prophets have said that He should be born in Bethlehem. May the Lord bring you in safety to that place, because you have had pity on the sick.'

It was already long past midnight. Artaban rode swiftly and Vasda, revived by the rest, ran eagerly over the silent plain and swam the river. She sped over the ground like a gazelle.

But the first beam of the sun fell on the temple as Artaban arrived, and he could find no trace of his friends. He dismounted and looked towards the west, to the edge of the desert. Jackals prowled in the low bushes, but there was no trace of the caravan of the Wise Men, far or near.

Under a pile of stones he saw a piece of parchment. He picked it up and read: 'We have waited past midnight and can wait no longer. We go to find the King. Follow us across the desert.'

Artaban sat on the ground and held his head in his hands. 'How can I cross the desert with no food and a tired horse? I must go back to Babylon, sell my sapphire and buy a train of camels and food for the journey. I may never reach my friends. God only knows.'

The Little Child

Dry and inhospitable mountain ranges rose around Artaban. He sat high on the back of his camel, rocking like a ship on the waves. Hills of treacherous sand heaped like tombs along the horizon. By day the heat was fierce; lizards vanished into the clefts of rocks. By night jackals barked in the distance and lions roared in the ravines. And it was cold. But Artaban moved steadily onward.

He rode past the orchards of Damascus and the Jordan valley, the dark groves of cedars and the Lake of Galilee, until he arrived at Bethlehem. It was the third day after the three Wise Men had come there and found Mary and Joseph and the young child Jesus, and had laid their gifts of gold, frankincense and myrrh at his feet.

The fourth Wise Man drew near the place the dying Hebrew had told him to go. He was weary but full of hope, bearing his ruby and pearl to give to the King. 'Now at last, I shall surely find him, though I am alone, and later than the others.'

The streets of the village seemed deserted. From the open door of a low, stone cottage he heard a woman singing softly. He went in and found a young mother hushing her baby to sleep. He asked if she had seen strangers from the East, and she told him that they had been in the village three days ago. A star had guided them to the place, they said, and they had found Joseph and Mary and their child, and had given him rich gifts.

She said the travellers had disappeared as suddenly as they had come, and Joseph had fled away with Mary and the babe that same night secretly. It was whispered

that they had gone to Egypt. 'It was all very strange,' she said, 'no one could understand it.'

As Artaban listened to her gentle voice, the child in her arms stretched out its rosy hand to touch the winged circle of gold on his breast. Artaban's heart warmed to this child who greeted him after his long and lonely journey. The young mother laid the babe in its cradle and set food before Artaban, the plain food of the poor, but gladly offered, and therefore refreshing to the soul as well as the body. Artaban took it gratefully; the child fell into a happy sleep, and a great peace filled the little room.

But suddenly the noise of a wild confusion filled the streets. Women screamed and swords clanged. The cry went up: 'The children! The soldiers of Herod! They are killing our children!'

The young mother's face went white with terror. She hugged her child to her bosom and crouched down in the darkest corner of the room, covering him with the folds of her robe, so he would not wake and cry.

Artaban got up quickly and stood in the doorway of the house. His broad shoulders filled the door.

The soldiers hurried down the street, their swords dripping with blood. At the sight of the tall man in the doorway, they stopped in surprise. The captain made to thrust him aside, but Artaban stood firm. His face was as calm as though he were watching the stars, and in his eyes shone that steady radiance that made leopards pause. He spoke in a low voice.

'I am all alone in this place, and I will give this jewel to the captain who will leave me in peace.'

He showed the ruby to the captain, who was amazed at its splendour. Lines of greed hardened around his mouth. He took the ruby from Artaban's hand.

'March on!' he cried to the soldiers. 'There is no child here!'

Artaban went back into the cottage. 'God of truth, forgive me!' he prayed.

But the woman, weeping for joy in the shadow of the room, said gently:

'Because you have saved the life of my

little one, may the Lord bless you and keep you, and make His face to shine upon you, and give you peace.'

The Plague

Artaban moved among throngs of men in Egypt, looking for traces of the little family that had come from Bethlehem. He found a faint trace under the sycamores of Heliopolis, but the family had gone on. He stood beneath the pyramids, and looked up into the vast face of the Sphinx, trying to read the meaning of the smile.

In Alexandria he went into the house of a Hebrew priest, who read the parchment on which the prophecies of Israel were written, and who said to him:

'Remember the king you are seeking is not to be found in a palace, nor among the rich and powerful. The light for which the world is waiting is a new light, that shall arise out of suffering. And the kingdom which is to be established forever is a new kingdom, the royalty of love.

I do not know how this shall happen, but I know this: those who seek him will do well to look among the poor and lowly.'

And so Artaban passed through lands where famine lay heavy and the poor had no bread. He lived in cities where the plague had caused many to fall sick, and, though he found none to worship, he found many to help. He fed the hungry, he clothed the naked, he healed the sick. And the years went by faster than the weaver's shuttle that flashes back and forth through the loom, while the invisible pattern grows.

It almost seemed as if he had forgotten his quest. Once, at sunrise, he took the pearl from its secret place in his bosom and looked at it, the last of his jewels. As he looked at it, a soft gleam with rays of blue and rose played on the surface of the pearl; it seemed to have in it the colours of

the lost sapphire and ruby. The pearl was growing brighter the longer it was carried close to the warmth of his beating heart.

The Pearl

Thirty-three years of Artaban's life had passed, and he was still a pilgrim. His hair that had once been darker than the cliffs of Zagros was now whiter than the snow that covered them in winter.

Tired and ready to die, but still searching for the King, he came to Jerusalem. He had been there many times before, wandering the lanes, with no news of the family from Bethlehem. Now it seemed to him that he must try again; this time he might succeed.

It was the season of Passover – the city was thronged with Israelites who were scattered through many lands, and who had come back to the temple for the Feast.

This day there was a great current of noise and excitement in the city, like the thrill that runs through the forest on the eve of a storm. There was a deafening clatter of sandals as the crowd surged towards the Damascus gate.

'Where are you going?' asked Artaban of an old man.

'We are going to Golgotha, outside the city, where there is to be an execution. Have you not heard? Two robbers will be crucified, and between them a man called Jesus of Nazareth, who has done many wonderful things. But the priests have sent him to the cross because he said that he was King of the Jews.'

How strongly these words struck the old heart of Artaban. They had led him for a lifetime over land and sea. The King had come; He had been denied, and now was about to die! Could this be the One who was born in Bethlehem thirty-three years ago, at Whose birth the Star had appeared?

Artaban followed the crowd with slow steps. Just outside the city a troop of soldiers came down the street, dragging a young girl with a torn dress. She looked at Artaban and threw herself at his feet.

'Help me!' she cried. 'I see the winged circle on your breast. I am also a daughter of the religion of the Magi. My father was a merchant from your land, but he is dead, and I am to be sold as a slave to pay his debts. Help me!'

Artaban trembled. It was the old conflict in his soul that had come in the palm grove and in the cottage at Bethlehem – the conflict between the hope of reward for his faith and the impulse of love. Twice the gift that he had wanted to save for the King had been given to man. This was the third trial, the final one.

One thing only was sure in his divided heart – to rescue this helpless girl would be a true deed of love.

He took the pearl from his bosom. Never had it looked so radiant. He laid it in the hand of the slave.

'Here is your ransom, my child. It is the

last of my treasures that I kept for the King.'

While he spoke the sky darkened; the earth shuddered like the breast of one who is struck with a mighty grief. The walls of the houses shook, and the soldiers fled in fear. But Artaban and the girl he had saved sat together beneath the wall of the city.

What had he to fear? The quest was over. He had given away his last treasure. Though it seemed the quest had failed, there was peace in the heart of Artaban. He knew that all was well because he had done the best he could, from one day to the next. He had not found the King in the flesh, but he knew that even if he could live his life over again, it could not be different from the way it was.

The ground shook with one more earthquake. A heavy tile, loosened from the roof, fell and struck the old man on the forehead. He lay breathless, his grey head resting in the lap of the young girl.

As she bent over him, a voice, still and small, came through the twilight, though there was no one there.

Then Artaban began to speak as if he were answering this voice:

'When, Lord, did I see You hungry and feed You, or thirsty and give You drink? When did I see You a stranger and take You in? Thirty-three years I have looked for You, but I have never met nor helped You, my King.'

He stopped. And the sweet voice came again; this time the words were very clear:

'Verily I say unto you, in as much as you have done it unto one of the least of my brethren, you have done it unto me.'

A calm radiance lit the face of Artaban, like the first ray of dawn on a snowy mountain peak. He breathed one long last breath of relief. His journey was ended. His treasures were accepted. The fourth Wise Man had found the King.

Afterword

Henry Van Dyke was born of Dutch stock in Pennsylvania in 1852. He grew up to be a pastor in churches, a poet and a story writer.

After studying at Princeton Theological Seminary, he became a pastor in churches in Rhode Island and New York City. It was in New York that his sermons were famous and well attended. *The Other Wise Man* was a Christmas sermon before it was a book. It has been translated into nearly all European languages and several Oriental languages.

When he was 32 he wrote *The Reality of Religion*, and after that, *The Blue Flower*.

This was a translation from the German poet Novalis, for whom the Blue Flower was a symbol for Poetry.

In 1900 Van Dyke settled at 'Avalon', his home in Princeton, New Jersey, where he lived for the rest of his life. He lived there with his wife and nine children, working as a Professor of English Literature and writing many books. He was also a keen fisherman and loved the Canadian wilderness, where he often took his sons camping. Van Dyke was at home with everyone, no one was a foreigner to him. One of his sons said, 'To him, romance was never distance; it was the vital quality of being alive among men and amid the unfathomable wonders of nature.'

President Woodrow Wilson appointed Van Dyke Minister to the Netherlands, but when he visited battlefields in France, Van Dyke wanted to be more active in helping the soldiers, so he joined the Chaplain Corps in the U.S. Navy. France thanked him by awarding him the Cross of the Legion of Honour, and Oxford University gave him an honorary degree.

Even after he retired, Van Dyke gave lectures to packed halls until he died in 1933. He and his wife celebrated their Golden Wedding Anniversary in 1931. Two years later, at dawn on an April day, he died after a brief illness. He was 81.

Van Dyke was a positive Christian, but never preachy. His parishioners and students appreciated his adventurous mind. He was handsome to look at, with a lively nature.

The Other Wise Man

Henry Van Dyke said in his Preface that the story came to him like a gift, and, 'It seemed as if I knew the Giver, though His name was not spoken.' The hero, Artaban, seemed to lead him, and to tell his own story. Van Dyke said he followed him.

Van Dyke was asked if it was right for Artaban to tell a lie, in the cottage in

Bethlehem, to save a child's life. He replied that a man might be forgiven more easily for a lie told to save another's life than for the cold sin of heartlessness. He felt that Artaban was always doing the best he could, and that 'there are some kinds of failure that are better than success.'

Though the story arrived like a welcome guest, Van Dyke, in order to clothe and feed him, had to go through many books of travel and ancient history to find the right details to plump up the story-guest.

The story has been condensed so that it can be read in one sitting. It is a story for Epiphany, twelve days after Christmas, and I have read it to our children on this day, even in their last year at school. We light a candle and begin.

The three Wise Men found the Christ Child at Epiphany, which is also known as Three Kings Day. 'Epiphany' is the Greek word for 'appearance' – the Child appeared to them on this day.

We have all known these 'appearances' in our lives, when the magic and meaning of something has made us notice it and wonder at it. It could be when a baby brother or sister is born, or a surprising present at Christmas, something that makes us catch our breath with the delight and surprise of it.

Especially now, when wonderful (wonder-full) things are not reported by newspapers and TV, it is more and more up to us to celebrate the open mysteries that make us wonder and hope. More than ever now, when success is measured in terms of money and power, we can discover that a noble life is worth more than gold.

It may look as though the other Wise Man failed in his aim to find the Christ Child – but did he really?

Look at what happened along the way – could he have said no?

The journey is as important as the goal. Everything the other Wise Man did brought more of Heaven here. Some kinds of failure are better than success.

Gabriel Bradford Millar

Other books from Hawthorn Press

All Year Round

Ann Druitt, Christine Fynes-Clinton, Marÿe Rowling.

Brimming with seasonal stories, activities, crafts, poems and recipes, this book offers an inspirational guide to celebrating festivals throughout the seasons. A sequel to *The Children's Year*, this book arises from the festivals workshops run by the authors at the annual *Lifeways* conference at Emerson College.

"The words are ours, the festivals are yours." This book encourages both adults and children to explore forgotten corners of the educational curriculum and to develop and adapt the various festivals to fit their own family traditions. The enthusiasm and colourful creativity with which this book is written is guaranteed to stimulate interest in the diverse and multiple joys of the seasons.

September 1995 200 × 250mm;
248pp; limpbound; colour cover; fully illustrated.

ISBN 1 869 890 47 7

Doctor Knickerbocker and Other Poems

Jane Grell.
Illustrations by Derrick Smith.

This book of participative poetry for children is an invaluable tool for inspiring self-expression in the classroom. Nothing can quite match Dr Knickerbocker's rich and riotous rhythm, movement and fun. This is a book that can transcend its classroom uses into the playground, the home and the wider community, transporting its participants to a land of African drums and rousing Caribbean rain.

Jane Grell was born and grew up on the Caribbean island of Dominica. Since 1976 she has been living and teaching in London, developing the oral story-telling of her heritage as a teaching style to aid bilingual learners in schools.

200 × 200; 48pp; paperback;
colour cover.

ISBN 1 869 890 65 5

Child's Play 3
Games for Life
for Children and Teenagers

Wil van Haren and Rudolf Kischnick.
Translated by Plym Peters and Tony Langham.

A tried and tested games book consisting of numerous ideas for running races, duels, wrestling matches, activity and ball games of skill and agility. Its clear lay-out, detailed explanations and diagrams and its indexing of games by age suitability and title makes *Child's Play* an invaluable and enjoyable resource book for parents, teachers and play leaders.

1994; 215 × 145mm;
126pp approx; paperback;
colour cover.

ISBN 1 869 890 63 9

The Lady and the Unicorn
Gottfried Büttner.
Foreword by Baruch Urieli. Translated by Roland Everett.

All great works of art stimulate the observer to ask questions. Here the author discusses the symbolism and real significance of the beautiful but enigmatic tapestries of the Paris Cluny Museum. Every work of art is rooted in culture and history, and their interpretation can provide valuable insights into the universal nature of the human being. Answering to a continuing interest in unicorn culture, Büttner concentrates on how the depiction of the unicorn bears relation to the development of the human soul.

July 1995; 297 × 210mm; 120pp; 16 colour plates.

ISBN 1 869 890 52 3

Festivals, Family and Food
Diana Carey and Judy Large.

An ideal companion to *Festivals Together*, this explores those numerous annual 'feast days' which children love celebrating. It was written in response to children and busy parents asking, "What can we do at Christmas and Easter? What games can we play? What can we make?"

Packed full of ideas on things to do, food to make, songs to sing and games to play, it's an invaluable resources book designed to help you and your family celebrate the various festival days scattered round the year.

The Observer

200 × 250mm; 216pp; limp bound;
colour cover; fully illustrated.

ISBN 0 950 706 23 X

Festivals Together
A Guide to Multi-cultural Celebration
Sue Fitzjohn, Minda Weston, Judy Large.

This is a resource guide for celebration, and for observing special days according to traditions based on many cultures. It brings together the experience, sharing and activities of individuals from multi-faith communities all over the world — Buddhist, Christian, Hindu, Jewish, Muslim and Sikh. Its unifying thread is our need for meaning, for continuity and for joy. Written with parents and teachers in mind, it will be of use to every school and family. Richly illustrated, there is a four page insert of seasonal prints by John Gibbs for your wall.

200 × 250mm; 224pp; limp bound; colour cover; fully illustrated.

ISBN 1 869 890 46 9

The Children's Year
Crafts and Clothes for Children and Parents to make
Stephanie Cooper, Christine Fynes-Clinton and Marÿe Rowling.

You needn't be an experienced craftsperson to create beautiful things! This charmingly illustrated book encourages children and adults to try all sorts of different handwork, with different projects relating to the seasons of the year. Over 100 potential treasures are described, including toys and games from all sorts of natural materials, decorations and even children's clothes.

200 × 250mm; 220pp; illustrated; sewn limp bound.

ISBN 1 869 890 00 0

If you have difficulties ordering from a bookshop you can order direct from

Hawthorn Press,
Hawthorn House,
1 Lansdown Lane,
Lansdown,
Stroud,
Glos.
United Kingdom,
GL5 1BJ

Telephone   0453 757040
Fax   0453 751138